POEMS AND THOUGHTS
OF A YOUNG PRIESTESS

POEMS AND THOUGHTS OF A YOUNG PRIESTESS

*Intense memories and revelations
of a woman looking for meaning*

By

ALEJANDRA RODRÍGUEZ PEÑA

Title: Poems And Thoughts of a Young Priestess

Editorial ITA S.A.S.
Published in the year: 2020
Number of pages: 111

Author: Alejandra Rodríguez Peña

Printed in: República de Colombia
Website: www.itabooks.com
ISBN: 978-958-52823-0-8

Cover design: © Editorial ITA S.A.S.
Cover photo: ©EvindART
Edition: © Editorial ITA S.A.S.

*To Absalón Rodríguez and to all of those
brave people who wish and work hard
to awake someday.*

DARK MATTER

Emptiness is the space where epiphanies merge.
Dark matter is the canvas that doesn't depict the art
because it contains itself but not everybody is able to see
it as anything that is truly essential.

Is just the closest concept that not only summarizes
the most imperatives actions that you would ever experience:
being and love, and their idyllic tantric synapse.

Empty yourself and you'll find yourself!
Don't be afraid! The only phantom is your most revered *trésor*
and is located carefully at the main chamber!

Empty yourself and you'll find you are love itself!
And when you find out who you are, I'll be waiting for you
to sway and sing the holy cosmology of music and dance.

Oh dear! Let's become humming birds and sip this
exquisite stupefying and mysterious charm from the original
flower of life!

The sacred grail is triumphantly awaiting for us
 at the striking banquet of holy existence…. and I...
I brought you a crown made of bay leaves and stars.

ABOUT POETRY

A both silent and tender revolution of love and consciousness.

It is my dance, my melody and poetry. And as Ferlinghetti used to say: poetry is madness and erotic bliss but also is the perfume of resistance. And I, I love it as I'd not love anything else but this truth.

CONTENTS

LA JOIE DE VIVRE

There was upon a time a girl who lived in a tiny cottage
house in the middle of a forest. A rich grove nearly as
dense as her bookshelves and cozy as the attic floor
where she used to draw, write, read, have some tea
during the afternoon and wine at night.

Her bliss was to admire the flowers which seemed to be
a succinct poem about the Universe while she waited for the stars
to begin with their ball in their silky, but shiny arrays as if they
were dancing the classical melodies she played in her house.

Was she waiting for a knight or prince to rescue her? No,
how could one feel trapped in such ecstatic paradise?
On contrary, she knew, that wondrous place had not only rescued
her but embraced her both impetuous and tender spirit and there,
she was not only free, but blissful and unapologetically herself.

And yes! she lived happy ever after! This is a love story as well.

BEING

Sometimes I feel in a *Liebesträume* dancing Listz, or
even drown in the Canon D of Pachelbel and sometimes
in the wild abandonment that causes this Nocturne in C-Sharp
Minor by Chopin.

And yes! I feel fortunate every time I allow myself to explore
the infinite faces of being a woman.
The unpredictable brush stroking the canvas where
my body organically paints.

TO SEVILLA

No! Neither Paris nor Rome or Verona, they are not the only cities for lovers. Come here and you will feel unapologetically in love.

This city is not only for lovers! Is a place that ignites love itself.

And yes... this is also *la vie en rose*! And as Shakespeare used to say: "*Vouchsafe* me yet your picture for my love".

TO BARCELONA

Brushstrokes of a city as emblematic as its architecture. May God bless your art as Gaudí has blessed you with his hands and brilliance my dear Barcelona!

How do I feel about you?
Just enthralled by the concinnity of your artful panorama and music of golden chords full of innovative Catalonian spirit.

VENICE, VERONA AND PARIS

In your streets I felt the beauty of your sadness.
Winter lights decorated your magnificence with tender diamond fractals of splendor.

I witnessed with glory the romantic promises of thousand lovers, surrendered to their joy. I felt enraptured by Vivaldi, Debussy and absolutely beguiled by the lines of the Shakespearean Tempest...

Alas... if they only had experienced my bliss they would have grasped the supremacy of their iconic real scenes full of grandeur.

The opulence of the Italian and French *milieu* would have been vanished by the vivified warmth of their dreams and enchanted by the potion of the present moment.

HUAIKA!

During the Spanish Conquest hundreds of families of indigenous people suicided massively in Huaika as a meaning of unconditional love and resistance.

Nevertheless, this territory is not only a remembrance of such staggering event in the Colombian history.

It is a magic gate for the Gods and Goddesses and stands for the balance of the Sacred Female and Male energies.

Come over to cast your demons, ignite your heart with the light of self-forgiveness and laud your divinity my friend!

The divine nature in me honors dearly your sanctity!

Ipqua, ipqua, ipqua Huaika!

REINVENTING THE PLAISIRS SOLITAIRES

Opera, ballet, literature and wine .. they should count as *plaisirs solitaires,* they are most definitely
a delicious orgasmic bliss that unleashes gracefully that part of us that's always grateful to be right here and right now.

And yes! This is not only good... but true and beautiful.

DANCE IS MY REVOLUTION

This is the way I speak, this is the way I scream
the deepest secrets inside of me.

This is the way I sing,
but also, this is the way I protest.

Stop bemusing! Let's ruin the tyranny in our heads.
Intoxicate the very demeaning feelings of grief and despair.

The void is always the best place to create! Shall we dance my
friend?

TO THE SACRED FEMININE

We are Hypathia, Zenji, all those women of science
that were burnt considered witches!

We are also Mary Ann Evans disguised as George Eliot
so she could publish her novels and Nadia Murad's fight
against sexual violence.

We are Marie Curie and Malala. We are muses, valkyries,
geishas, priestesses.

Sensitive, bounteous and trailblazing yet sybaritic, sultry
and fierce fairies.

An ode to the spirit of creation, the same scent of music,
the delightful whisper of thousand *eurekas*!

Epiphanies connected to the source of divinity.
Passionate daughters of the anarchy of love!

Yes! We deserve unbeatable, unbearable, unconditional
love and devotion of all the gods because we are goddesses.

No! we do not apologize for being ourselves, we know what we
are made of! And our sacredness honors your sanctity!

TO THE SACRED MASCULINE

He's the king of kings without crowns or armors,
knows how to rule without commanding!

Knows he's part of everything, yet everything is part of him,
is silently committed and loudly devoted to the Light

His scent guides me to the infinite pleasures of life and makes me
find both my power and peace.

He is the unbounded space where music dances and sings
her most glorious chant.

The muses eulogize His awakening
with zither sounds and place laurels tenderly upon His head.

INSPIRED BY "BATH TIME IN GAZA" BY EMAD NASSAR

A man and his two daughters playing, enjoying water
while they still have it, feeling the celestial presence of those
they love meanwhile they still have each other...
being fully aware about the grievous scenery...

Truth is only love sets us free! It melts the barricades of
disaster and grows from the deepest darkness,
because it looks for the light and overthrows tenderly
the tyranny of the impossible and the unknown.

Love allows us understand we don't need neither armors
nor weapons to face the hardest adversities. Love is the means,
 the process and purpose.

And Life without love... is that execrable panorama on back of
this photograph.

Only love sets us free!

TO OUR PASSIONS

Because no matter what... passions are our muses
and there is something about us always looking for them!

If we didn't have a body to incarnate them
our divine tantric halo will always embrace them.

They are ours, as the oxygen belongs to the air
and as our liberty belongs to the dance of their music
while we live and pass away.

INSPIRED BY "LIFE IS BEAUTIFUL"

So her husband escaped from the Nazis for a second and said by their speakers: ."_Good morning princess, last night I dreamt about you, we went to the movies and you were wearing that pink dress I like so much, I only think about you , you are always in my heart!".

Suddenly, she forgot about the fact that she was in a concentration camp in Auschwitz. Now, she was in that beautiful pink dress dancing Offenbach: *Belle nuit ô nuit d'amour!* with her lover.

And yes! Also there, due to the liberating power of love, she realized that she was unbearably happy and life was certainly beautiful.

WASHINGTON 1976 (TO MY DAD)

Admirable subtlety, a walking and always open library with the wisdom of the most valuable and ancient treasures. An assortment only as big as his both generous and noble heart.

Enchanting sense of humor always accompanied by a very classy grimace, a never-ending desire for justice, a fervent defender of the glory of knowledge, music and silence. That was my dad!

Last year when my family and I were on our way to US, Luciana, my 4-year-old niece asked me if we could tell the pilot to stop the airplane for a second so we could visit him...

Truth is my friends: every time I look at the sky, I see him
 in his embellished clothes convincing God and his House of Lords, with bounteous shrewdness: we had enough of war, ignorance and poverty.

DANCE WILL MAKE US

Value the unspoken language of the soul tattooed in
the organic memory of your body. Cortázar used to say:
"come sleep with me, we won't make love, love will make us".

Let me tell you my friend, the alchemy of music will make you,
it will tear the routine down; it will drown your fears and
paint your heart's chamber while watering the forgotten seeds
with tender drops of redemption.

Love is its melody, and yes it will make you too.

ODE TO DANCE

A lighthouse for the passionate castaways,
a billion fireflies igniting the path where tender larks build
hanging bridges so pedestrian dreamers can survive.

The vibrant electric memoirs of achieving what's both possible
and impossible through our Dionysian and Apollonian nature.

A plausible derision against condemnation. Rejoice and revelry in
the middle of chaos. Terpsichore's DNA activated in our blood.

Butterflies coming out of a very astounding music box liberating
the melody of our deepest inner truths.

RED

Divine intoxication of life, sacred fuel of passionate and condensed desires!

Explosive *ardeur* of chaotic abundance, you are the spirit
of the hallowed vibrant Golden Fleece!

Sweet *mare magnum* of creation: I just can't have enough of
you!

SOME GIRLS

Some girls are rare like fire lilies, delicate like pansies, strong like the roots of redwoods, unforgettable like the scent of jasmine and hard to find like four leaf clovers.

IN DEFENSE OF WHOLE PRINCESSES

Stop pigeonholing princesses! Not all of them are the depthless weak women people think they are. Some of them are erudite, exude poise, strength and grace.

They are a perfect collage that integrates the virtuosity of the goddesses. I'm pleased to say I'm gracefully surrounded by them.

SAP OF SEQUOIAS

Absolute ecstasy is what I feel surrounded by these loving red and green guardian angels of the earth.

My heart belongs to the forest as my mind to the ancient artful libraries!

My body, to the dancing foliage of trees and my spirit to the endless majestic melody of the Universe.

This is not only good, but true and mesmerizingly beautiful!

KNOWLEDGE OF THE SELF

Collect moments and lessons out of the comfort zone. We only live once and the world is endless, diverse, illustrious, fascinating and pertinacious.

The uncertainty is the key that keeps us enraptured by the iconic fragrances of love.

Love the desire of exploring more than discovering. The sacred fleece is the path, the pursuit, the mystery, the courage and the adventure.

Life's force drifts in the kisses floating from my hands to yours. They wait for you to receive them even though I don't know you.

YOUNG EYES

I walk around the world with eyes full of amazement,
joy and gratitude because nature, art and astronomy
nourish my soul with vibrant doses of a spiritual awakening
no church could have ever given me.

And this is my paradise, my home, a spot full of being rather than
doing. A *claire-obscure* Canaan decorated subtly with blithesome
constellations, far away from the distracting *kitsch* griffin of
chaotic dusty *vaudevillian* highways.

And yes! As Griffith used to say: If all mankind could look
through that telescope it would change the world.

LA DAME ET LA MER

Farewell my lovely ! Before the falcon takes over make sure you have a big sleep.

Farewell my lovely sweet lady in the lake! Please do not turn this into a long goodbye!

TO MY BELOVED FRENCH READER

Jouer à gagner ! Danser avec les mélodies océaniques de la plage sans remords!

Guérir avec la joie de nôtre enfant intérieur!
Vivre avec le cœur plein de bonheur !

Ça c'est jouer à vaincre sans avoir lutter!

Jouer à gagner nous-mêmes.

We'll play to win! We'll dance to the melodies of the ocean in the beach without remorse!

We'll heal with joy our inner child!
We'll live with our hearts full of fortune!

And that! Is to play and win without having ever fought!
We'll play to win ourselves.

BE BRAVE MILADY

Incarnate Alexandria's library with all of its mystery,
be the warrioress and the priestess of your own sanctuary.

Honor the sacred grail, be the melodious ambrosial pure maiden
who plays joyfully with the unicorns;

Be also dexterous both erudite and fierce enough to roar
whenever treacherous minds find it hard to understand your
sanctity.

BACK TO YOU MOTHER

Back to you Mother Nature, to your ground full of sense, to your colorful embrace full of red and green. Nearly naked because your love is uncovered and I need to be showered with your holy sap!

Then, just dress me up with the petals of your divine wisdom. Because in a world full of flimsy bonds your love lasts forever.

And as Bukowski used to say: "(..) I don't have time for things that have no soul"

WOMEN AND WAR

There is nothing more nonsensical than war. We have never been the owners of this earth. Borders divide nations to make people fall in the trap that some of us are superior than others.

Especially governments involved in wars, couldn't care less about people and Mother Earth. They want us to believe some of us are heroes and some others villains, brainwashing us with religion, cultural, gender and race superiority.

But yes! The flower that blossoms during the adversity is the rarest and the most beautiful of all and absolutely yes! There's definitely nothing in the world a girl who loves her family couldn't do to protect them.

Of course! Women can be delicate as butterflies, the most elegant swans but also fierce and wise as the wildest of lions with both eagle vision and angelical wings.

TO THE QUEEN OF PEOPLE'S HEARTS

In a world where life does not seem to matter, mostly ruled by greed, ambition and bigotry, you lead from your abundant both generous and compassionate heart.

You showed us how love could break those enormous barriers built by treacherous minds that don't allow us see what's really essential.

FOR THE EMANCIPATION OF LOVE

How can we love somebody if we do not want their freedom?
How can we be ourselves when the other one cannot be?
Love means: how can I help you so you can be!

STRENGTH AND BALLERINAS

People see you up there and think you're fragile,
but they are wrong! If you let a brick fall, it might break
easily; nevertheless, when what you let fall is a feather it will not
only dance through the air as if it was its partner but also it will
land delicately as if it was stroking the floor gracefully.

Thus, the compact brick is the weak one just like
those rigid minds who associate violence with power!
Today is the moment to redefine the word "strength".

CLAIMING THE SACREDNESS OF THE BODY

From Goddess Hestia, I comprehended, my body was a sanctuary of divinity I should honor providing it the best kind of treatment possible in order to address good inner and outer health.

From Artemis, I understood I could love my body for what it was able to do when it was truly aligned to my goals and passions.

From Aphrodite, I realized our senses were a powerful source of self-knowledge as well as both ecstasy and profound bliss.

From Athena, I learned to love it since it is an instrument to witness nature and observable facts.

Therefore, I can't neither ban nor decry it. How can we hate something so both sublime and sacred? Why do we consider it is unacceptable to show its splendor?

Why can't we be grateful for this miracle called body?

NATURE, MY EDEN, MY HOME

Shush! Listen to the symphonies of the forest, the sweet percussions of bird's flutter when they haunt silky vibrant flowers.

The both sibilant and howling sound of wind when it wallows delicate branches during spring time;

Stroke the grass while its *verdeur* suffocates your sins purifying your soul with holy petrichor.

Dive with my spirit in the tender rivers of innocent love while water lilies perfume your existence.

Now relish the sacred sap from the tree of life and find me there, where the essential comes visible, when you are dreaming yet you could not be more awake.

In nature I find my medicine, my freedom; in art, my emancipation. And that is all I need, that magnificent abundance where I can be.

WHILE PROMENADING LONDON

Two days ago, promenading one of my favorite cities in the world, I witnessed an attempt of suicide and how all of a sudden a random person threw a life vest to a man who was in the water while other, seconds after, jumped out of the bridge risking his life to save another.

Perhaps the most important people we'll ever meet are completely strangers we met by accident. What they don't know is when they do their magic thousands of children stare at them.

I'm also talking about you and I, hearts that become inspired,
a part of humanity in which we suddenly, by a sort of serendipity
or miracle we all can rely.

If you are one of those people all I want to say is: sorry for all those who never see you: I love you, because
when you were saving other people, you also were saving me.

Thank you!

BIRDS AERIAL DANCE ROUTINE WITH CHOPIN'S *FANTAISIE IMPROMPTU* OP 66

Perhaps birds learn to fly so they can dance stroking the *fantasie* of the skies.

Probably they hug the wind, but they can't catch it, so it becomes their eternal love for one only loves with whom one can be free.

It might be that they fell for the vast immensity and its astounding surprise! *Chapeau* my little revolutionary creatures. Your creativity is my freedom and your unexpected *rendez-vous* at the window a misty sweet hope is to me.

TO THE SKEPTICAL

Look around and even upside down!
How can't you believe in magic, don't you see it is everywhere?

ECSTASY

This! Fireworks of serotonin, dopamine and oxytocin bursting gracefully in the canvas of existence. Nature and art... my permanent fuels,

My both real and surreal necessities. Sweet overwhelming odes I cannot stop listening.

A FREE WOMAN

A free woman is quite the opposite of an easy one! That for sure!

She's a bird dressed like a very vibrant butterfly!

A very precious stone you can admire but never possess.
Don't tell her to go to your place, don't ask her to be yours!

 She hates cages. She loves open real nature, conversations
about books because knowledge makes her freer.

Wine at night, an afternoon tea, Rachmaninov and Debussy's
soirées perhaps!

Real things, neither your car nor your watch. If she was a dance
pose her name would be *port de bras*!

it seems you want to hold her but all of a sudden everything just
makes sense when you release. Let her be!

YOU FIRST MILADY!

I want you to promise me you'll never sacrifice the depth of your heart, your blissful spirit and the width of your mentality so you can be in the comfortable place others call social correctness and normality.

¿IF WE ALL HOLD HANDS WHO IS GOING TO USE WEAPONS?

If we only knew our differences instead of harming us, enrich us. If we could only see that there is no progress at all if it does not take into account our health and natural resources.

If we could only admit the highest act of love is taking care of the other one's rights even though apparently, we have it all.

If we could only understand that outside the trap of fear and submission there is life!

Oh, this world would be peaceful and everyone freer!

BECOME WHAT YOU DREAM

Transform and renew as many times as you need, enjoy the creative process of getting closer to what sets your soul on fire.

Love yourself enough to become what you love and do not allow anybody to stop you, it is a day less instead of a day more.

Today's opportunity will never come back again. Distractions disappear when every day is a new date with your dreams. And that one! That's the most important *rendez- vous!*

Enjoy the blissful elixir of actions until they become the holy victorious chant.

SEA PRAYER

Mighty, almighty sea, devour my sins
with the mystic foams of your sanctity!

Sweet holy sun open gates of sacred wisdom
aligning my will, my thoughts and heart.

TO MY BLACK ANCESTORS

Black means depth, black means genius, black is anarchy and alchemy!

You turned slavery into art, you showed the tyrants how
your spirit was bigger and stronger than any chain or sword.

You put the Caribbean and Pacific seas in the hips of Colombian women so the world knew the powerful yet very subtle cumbia.

Your braids were your crowns, the only ones ever made to show others their way to their own freedom.

Thank you forever! And if nobody has ever told you this: I'm proud of you, I love you.

SOIRÉE OF SPIRITUAL INTEGRATION

Own the night, its gold mysteries and emerald *follia*,
wear it as your favorite dress.

Let God be famished, become his banquet's most delicious
v*ichyssoise* with every second of your existence,

Allow your virtuosity decorate his gardens with *dent de lion's*
mystical feathers.

Incense your hair with laurel leaves and flood his kingdom
with the triumphant march of the Goddess.

THE INSURGENT ART OF BEING A FREE WOMAN

Society tells women, we have to find physically strong, good hearted, intelligent, rich men and never show any kind of strength because they will run away from us. What society wants is mentally, emotionally, physically and financially handicapped women!

Unleash that woman society is so afraid of and feel how your partner is absolutely complimentary instead of another necessity. See how you start to appreciate your growth by not allowing less than what you deserve.

Protect your body as the temple of the goddess it is,
giving it the best kind of treatment in order to keep it healthy.
Teach them a lesson, start reading enough history so you understand their *modus operandi*!

And love yourself so much they stop profiting from yourself doubt. That insurgent art my dear is sublime and unapologetically beautiful.

THE DIVINE INSIDE OF US

We are used to mediocrity, to believe the divinity is outside of us, we believe everything is disconnected and we have been told we need to have faith for we can't see that divinity. That's a trap!

Let your spirit burn the structures of that web and free yourself. You are divine and the highest powers grow inside of you. Believe me: you are everything you need!

BEATRIX HAND

Do not be afraid, close your eyes, hold my hand, in our hearts is neither cold nor dark, trust these words I am as you are.

TO THE MOON

How could you shine so bright if darkness wasn't deep enough? Bless me with your pale diamond dress, and comb my hair with the stories of the noblest stars before you perish in the arms of the golden sun!

BE KIND

In a world full of rivals, let's cooperate; Let's be brothers and sisters. Let's redefine society together. Stop saying we love if we don't care!

Stop dreaming and start doing! If one grows from the inside, we all do!

Today is time to connect and intertwine our roots of love so we all become stronger! We need that strength to face adversities, to face life itself!

Let's be kind to ourselves, to our divine goddess Mother Nature and the others, understand we all have suffered enough.

Our differences make us learn more about everything and each other enrich us profoundly. We are not disconnected!

Let's enjoy the both sacred and revolutionary art of being ourselves. Accept and embrace that marvelous endeavor!

A DESPERATE WISH

Even though everything and everyone will perish
Allow your passions immortalize the ephemeral moment of your existence.

Feel how you become a vibrant hope one of those chimerical summer nights when lovers wish upon a star!

DON'T STOP DANCING *MA BELLE*

Dance until you feel one with music and culture, dance until your chains fall off, dance to heal the wounds of slavery! Dance to melt the tyrant dictatorship of your head. Dance until the empire that moves you becomes the one of life and freedom. Dance until Caliban turns into Ariel! Dance until you flow with the symphony of everything and feel prepared to leave your body peacefully so you can free your soul.

Don't stop dancing *ma belle*!

TO GODDESS PELE

Let's make bliss and enjoyment permanent states of mind by feeling and incarnating the strength of the bursting volcanic energies of creation. Raise from the depths of tender seas, become fertile and fruitful earth and puff yourself up with subtle strokes of delicate winds!

TO VIVIANA

When she loses her fears, she achieves her dreams and we all win because her smile fills with hope all the most grieving hearts. I call her muse, one of those Valkyries who represent nations and stand for power and the most both noble and essential virtues!

A DANCER'S PRAYER

Thank you music, body and life! Thanks Divinity, for another day I can dance. Thanks for your Spirit that makes people create intimate moments of art.

TOGETHER WE WON'T ONLY GO FURTHER!

Together we won't only go further , we'll get stronger and we'll also understand our nature, where everyone can be! And that, that's my happiness, to see you growing and glowing as if the only matrix affecting you was our compassionate roots of acceptance, contemplation and understanding.

Let's heal together and help more and more people comprehend what love can do, let's become ladders so everyone can achieve their purest dreams, let's fill this world with hope and the courage of chasing our divine glory holding hands. Let's tumble down the barricades of fear so everyone can be.

TRUE DEVOTION AND COMMITMENT

Promise yourself you are going to discover what your body is capable of before you die!

Promise yourself no matter what you think you are, you are never going to stop being kind!

Promise yourself you are going to drown your anxiety, fears and ignorance in the so many interesting adventures and books there are.

Promise yourself you are going to work hard on keeping your temple strong, flexible, well-nourished and protected as the most valuable wealth you were given.

Promise yourself, you will defend what you have always been dreaming! Promise yourself you'll always see in others the roots of Divine.

Promise yourself you are going to treasure what you have earned with discipline and determination.

Find in knowledge, nature and arts the holy source of true pleasure, connection and redemption.

ABOUT DREAMING

Yes! Be a dreamer, but more than that, be somebody who works every single day of this incredible life for making those dreams come true.

Bury very deep your fears down by understanding the steps you have to make towards what you want. Study them cautiously and with that same awareness, with that eagle spirit of yours, trust yourself!

Now, start the journey and believe me: you only fear what you don't comprehend!

WHAT DO YOU FEEL WHEN YOU DANCE?

I feel free, grateful, powerful, and delicate but most of all very certain of this passion where music seduces every pore and part of my body. I wonder if the ground feels perhaps how alive I feel meanwhile.

MYSTICAL EVIDENCE

For some, she was this enigmatic riddle, one nobody has ever been able to solve. A cruel *finis afriçae*, a point of no return for mortal minds. For others, she was this always accessible garden where everybody could easily find comfort. A peaceful Eden, the same scent of *atharaxia*, something very contrary to the fatal labyrinths that lead to doom. An ethereal mystical evidence of a summer equinox during a winter's solstice.

CONFESSIONS AT FOUR MINUS 10

She's barefoot quite often and her messy rebellious hair only calms down a little bit when she starts to roll and tangle it. This usually happens around 5 PM when she becomes more and more enthralled by the first sip of a hot rose tea, sat down in an old-fashioned afternoon tea place, reading some good old French or English book God knows why people took for granted!

ABOUT HER BLISS

The dance floor for her is something very similar to Olber's night sky paradox, a place where everything is light. Her favorite dress is one she's still sewing with her virtues, you can see it shining every moment someone invited her to dance.

IN LOVE OR NOTHING AT ALL

No! Believe me, she's not an extrovert, perhaps sometimes it seems she talks to much, but maybe and I bet you haven't realized this yet, she unfolds spontaneously only talking about things she's really passionate about because she's sincere and true to her soul. She's in love or nothing at all!

She's got very few friends including the papers where she draws, writes and the dance floor where she unleashes quite often, and let's not talk about the punching torso in her terrace she only stops boxing to see the sunset in the chaotic city while listening to Chet Baker.

She's friends with them, bewilderingly, because they have witnessed the alchemy of seeing her mystically turning into this inextinguishable fire she is now!

Those unanimated instruments have seen her in love and even nothing at all, and she has perceived them as the priests and priestesses of a temple where she goes to become a complete different and enhanced version, one nobody has ever seen before.

Believe me… she's in love or nothing at all.

HIM

So you see him, sat down singing like a goldfinch that flew all the way back from the Thames river to wreck down these walls build up by ego with his both subtle and divine flutter showing it takes just one single gesture of sweetness to melt the hardest of all structures.

And all of a sudden, as if his golden song was a lullaby, an otherworldly one, a flashback of the sweetest memories of London started to come back.

Thanks for your existence! May the Universe bless your hands receiving what brings you the most unbearable joy! Thank you forevermore.

ABOUT WOUNDS

Life will keep on breaking you down until you realize is through your wounds where light comes in. Do not become harder, become sweeter and kinder. Be brave enough to do so! Allow the beauty of your story and dreams fulfill the deepest of your darknesses with holly radiant drops of hope.

TO YOU MEN!

Men! I love you to the bone! And I want you free from the patriarchal barricades that told you to "man up" when we both, men and women were meant to be a team.

This "man up" idea has made you become the population that actually commit more suicide in the whole world. I want you free to become the artists who actually have always been taken for granted because "men" don't do that.

I want you to say more "I love you" and never be afraid of showing vulnerability, because it actually requires an incredible strength. I want you free to understand you don't defend nations but just the elite's interests.

I want you to understand that deep down, that's what the war and "superior" mentality is all about. I want you free to focus on solutions that benefit us all.

I want you to realize that there are not enemies rather than our own thoughts. I want you free to comprehend we all need to be heard and our first and most urgent necessity is to heal our minds.

Men! I want you to admit that progress doesn't mean you have to destroy the lands and enslave other people as well as other creatures because society told you to "man up".

Men! I want you to be free and I feel you! That's why I am who I am, because love couldn't be another thing than wanting you to be free, cared and understood.

Let's hold hands and wake up together!

THE VEIL

Very contrary to what society established and believed, the veil for her was not meant to hide her hair or physical beauty.

She used to wear it with her sisters every time one of them needed to accept and reconnect to their own divinity in a very glorious ritual. One, in which they stroked their lips with heavenly honey of compassion to bless each other and themselves.

Then, they shared a cup of jasmine tea to immortalize in their palates how peace tasted like; and last but not least, they put their hallowed veils with reverence incarnating the mistresses of forgiveness they had always been.

ABOUT INNER WORK

The more you mature, the more you start treasuring what you have earned with plenty of effort, especially when it is directly linked to your inner growth and healing.

Why is it? Because it showed you who you really are and perhaps it took you years, tears and lessons. Hence, stop justifying yourself with the "I'm like this and I can't change" thought!

What if you don't know who you are because you don't want to get out of the jail you built up for yourself! Emancipate now from that false belief!

What if you stop being self-destructive and start appreciating what you have learned throughout the years!

Give yourself the place you deserve because nobody else is going to give it to you if you don't do it.

Well, that's my definition of dignity. Stop chasing low-priced and shallow things when life has showed you're inestimable!

SPONTANEOUS POEM TO CHOPIN'S NOCTURNE B IN FLAT MINOR OP 9 #1

The heavenly orchard of everything in your mind , Eden's sweet scented flowers in your hands, the mystical agony of the not so creative mankind.

Melancholic bliss, love itself, how the impossible collides gracefully. From beautiful ruins you built up a pompous now virtuous Versailles!

GREAT SUPREME GODDESS

At the end, Mother Nature, the Great supreme Goddess, who has been providing us generously more than we need throughout the days, is going to shake our hearts over and over again until there's no greed inside of them,

Until we understand she doesn't belong to us since love is more about caring instead of belonging,

Until we understand we can't say we love each other but still kill among ourselves while destructing her and her glory while we label that as the progress of our civilization.

She's going to shake us over and over again until we empty ourselves from false beliefs of superiority and segregation.

She's going to shake us over and over again until we understand we need to move towards learning and awareness no matter how hard it seems.

She's going to shake us over and over again until we understand subtlety and generosity avoid the hardest tempests, turning off the most indomitable fires as the salt of our passions brings life to our dreams melting the ice of our fears that paralyzed us for so long.

She's going to shake us over and over again until we understand the strongest one is the one who stands in the battle without any other armor rather than their own skin!

She's going to shake us over and over again, until we start giving our hands not to harm, for everyone is vulnerable, but to find in the scented gardens of love and unity, our most sublime source of strength.

TO BABY LUCIANA

My little fairy of prosperity, my sweet rainbow during tempestuous days, my joyful ballad when I couldn't be more sad. An ode to the most glorious times, the veiled virtues hidden for humankind. My everything and so much more! Cherub's graceful relieving beauty and Seraphim's forever both melodious and victorious chant!

FLOW FOR YOU ARE WATER, SHINE FOR YOU ARE GOLD

Society told us strength was related to avoiding our individuality and emotions. Today more than any other day, let's open our hearts and find the real strength in there! Let's embrace who we are and start that process of supreme revelation. the most sacred work of art. Let's Inspire others to break their chains!

ONENESS

Become the free spirit of the present moment and bless your temple, while you feel it gets so tender you can leave it! Understand God and Goddess are one everywhere! One with everything, one with you!

TO HIM

Brilliant brain and beautiful teeth, he reminds me of Chopin, his piano, his nocturnes   full of melancholy and their constant invitation to understand life. He's like million fireflies shining bright when you're lost in a very deep and cloudy night!

He's thousand winged golden falling stars willing to guide you while showing you the path. The most compassionate suggestion from the divine order to appreciate and embrace the value of knowledge and mostly the unknown, a remedy for the grieving and ignorant humankind!

TO DEISY AND DIANA

And suddenly God created these two virtuous women to summarize the beauty of the Goddess of all creation. He fell deeply for what he did once and immediately he replicated his art making sure both of these lordly creatures could complement the never-ending grace of the other one.

TO MY LITTLE FAIRY

How can somebody be human and dare to love you! Even though it is not allowed for me to feel it, I do and I prefer to become another creature, one very blessed with your otherworldly magic, one very willing to appreciate you in all your dimensions profoundly. I couldn't be this better if you weren't here, in this planet.

Thank you with every atom of the universal serendipity that brought me to you. Thank you forevermore my living little Lucy in the sky with diamonds.

COURAGE

Unleash the wings of creativity and incarnate the essence of the unknown, understand it, dance it and you'll fear no more! The same power of cosmos where everything is connected and flowing inside of you! Dance the sacred music of this Universe in motion so you feel the power of unity. Integrate it and stay in this state of permanent glory, from now on everything will shine for you!

TANTRIC DANCE

When it seems all lost, dance and your body will speak the mystical languages of God when he's one with the goddess! Recover the sacred connection when one makes love to life. The end is just the perfect time to give birth to creation. Embrace the experience!

Become the divine technology of the Universe intertwined with the golden threads and scents of the Holy Spirit of everything! Take my hand and my seeds, let's witness the symphony of life while we become the main characters but also the authors behind this story.

UNDERSTAND

Understanding will allow you to feel comfortable during the uncomfortable. Every time you choose to comprehend, you detach gently from the ideas of impossibility. Bend! But most of all: flow! And if you don't: study! Until you integrate what you wish to know naturally. Be one with it!

Do as Wright brothers who didn't know that flying was impossible and achieved it anyways! Do as the so many scientifics who had the cure and invention in mind years before they proved them! Embrace the unattainable.

Never lose the capacity for amazement and its purity! Those brand-new eyes always willing to appreciate the totality and beauty of the unknown while waiting patiently finding rejoice in the journey of learning. Ulysses will suddenly meet her beloved Penelope realizing they were never really apart!

All the roads lead to your lover, all of them lead to you!

TO YOU

He told her he was scared of not being enough for her, so she hugged him and told him they were a team, and once one becomes part of it, there's no competition at all! For both are complimentary and hold hands to be stronger to deal with difficulties and face life.

And yes! She was contagiously impetuous, biblically brave. But it takes more courage to admit whenever one feels vulnerable. At the end of the day we all are and also too afraid to confess it.

ELEGY AT 11:11

How dare you say I don't know you! Your body has enough freckles to narrate the most epic stories to our sons and grandchildren, but you are too much into that damn "anarchy" thing that paradoxically it doesn't allow you to settle down with me. You ruined my life and its whole meaning.

I curse the day I fell for the sky and decided to become an astronomer, while God made you the synthesis of my whole Universe! Alpha Persei Cluster is in your cheeks, Cassiopea in your neck, Beta Commae Berenices in your nose, Castor and Pollux in your left shoulder while Collinder 399 lays gracefully in your back!

I know you better than you would ever know yourself and I hate it. I loathe the way you straight your hair and dye it blonde and the magnificent rebellious art of nature that turns it red and curly each 28 every month! It reminds me of the sun's nuclear fusion! It terrifies me looking at the sky during starry nights. I do hate all this as much as I ardently love you.

LETTER TO THE ASTRONOMER

Dear astronomer!

Emancipate yourself from that imperialistic perspective of love. Stars are beautiful for they decorate the infinite firmament with their unique glow! They are not just some other chandelier of that opulent house of yours.

For the same reason, please never try to put a ballerina in a music box. Do not dare to possess what you say you adore unless you wish to see how melancholy poisons gradually her delicate soul.

Do not profane the Universe you once told me you loved.

Freely no one's property,

The ballerina.

MY LOVER

The Supreme Spirit of my passions, he is my only lover! What I breathe meanwhile He is possessing me, the divine nature that connects me to the source from every single of my senses. No man has ever given me that feeling of becoming Goddess while celebrating God in the banquet of creation.

MY SANITY AND *FOLLIA*

Dance is my sanity, my sweetest *follia,* the hidden language of my soul. The wind, heat, water and earth, sparkles of electricity highlighting both my destiny and dreams, the bioluminescence of my blood.

IN MEMORIAM: PROFESSOR ABSALÓN RODRÍGUEZ DÍAZ, MY DEAREST UNCLE

Before he was born, the glorious alchemical forces chose the best virtues from all angelic realms, Mother Mary store them all very subtle in just one man's heart!

Suddenly, Gabriel told my grandmother in dreams. Oh, my dear! If you only knew you are the vehicle of what every single family needs!

You are carrying who is going to be a father of peace, what we call in Hebrew: a true charming prince!

If this wasn't enough, his first name will evoke what in Latin stands for freedom, with divine actions heavens will show you all their love!

Throughout the days, he did not only become the best man, but an accomplished scientist and teacher, an impeccable father and husband.

One of those people whose both passionate and brilliant art enrich souls and beautify lives with seeds of hope for all humankind!

One day, before he left, he told me: never worry for a man, they will all die, embrace your passions and certainly everything will certainly be alright!

Yesterday, he returned to the arms of the Beloved, where he was sent, the same source of Light, the holy wondrous divine tent!

LOOK FOR WHICH IS AND IS NOT APPARENT! *FACTA NON VERBA!*

How many times did we believe in words instead of actions, How many times did we keep on doing the same because we had a poor relationship with ourselves?

Let us assess love, friendship, change, promises and commitment based on actions starting with ourselves. Eventually others will delude us only if we keep on caring about receiving what does not depend on us.

I hope you never have unrequited bonds and if you do, feed self-awareness and esteem, treasure loyalty incarnating it! Surrender to the charming fragrances of your passions and you will never feel betrayed.

And believe me! At the end of the day, all the roads lead to you!

THE KINGDOM OF MY BELOVED

Anywhere I can create, I find my Beloved, in the piece of paper where I write odes to express how profoundly grateful I am, He is in the pencils I approach and pretend to grasp His beauty and in the patterns that connect the Universe to our nature.

He is the nakedness of my vulnerabilities, in the salty lessons inside my tears, in the tasty sap of my feelings. In the power of my will and thoughts and inside the wounds that opened to find their way to the Light.

Life is getting lost in His kingdom while at the end we realize He has always been dancing with us everywhere. My Beloved doesn't judge me for He is an artist, and just through Art I find the way to my soul and my Beloved too.

WITHOUT LABEL OR APPARENT ROUTE

Embrace uncertainty, what is unpredictable, incorporate the nature of life itself and flow like the autumn leaves that once belonged to the tree, but now dance freely in the wavy frenetic breath of the wind without inquiring where they go.

THE DIFFERENCE BETWEEN THE WARRIOR AND THE PRIEST

Do not hide from life, allow yourself to feel, observe what you do spontaneously with your emotions. Train yourself to tame them, master your basic instincts, make them all source of divine power and they will become your dearest alibis. This is going to be the hardest lesson you will ever learn: the difference between the warrior and the priest.

TO KNOW THE UNKNOWN

Become the instrument of art itself! Dance! Intertwine with Solomon while you become his keys, secrets and wisdom. Surrender to the sacred undisclosed knowledge of the Divine for you are one with it.

Do not forget to undress yourself from the heavy clothes of fears and illusion, immortalize the tantric bliss of the present moment in the sincerity and delicacy of your movement and skin.

Stroke and explore the vastness of the Universe in motion, the Sacred Chamber where everything is Light while it opens your mind showing you infinite open doors.

MY HORN OF PLENTY

Because time doesn't come back and if I had to die tomorrow, I'd dance until I heal what there's still missing. I'd dance with all my gratitude for the miracle of life and the fortune of having done what I loved the most.

And yes! There isn't something more unconditional than our passions, solitude turns into our sky, the *atelier* and canvas where we can fly freely naked, our stage and refuge!

GLORIOUS TANTRIC NIGHTS!

Wherever I go I see you my Lover! During glorious nights I celebrate our meeting, the most desired *rendez-vous,* your Spirit invites me to transcend my mortality a la *tombée* du jour! My body is prepared for it has received the essence of Mother Nature, my biggest pleasure is to praise our holy custody every soirée with every single atom of mine, for my physicality gives tribute to You and the Supreme Goddess.

THE GREATEST HONOR!

The greatest honor is not to be loved, but to love! The one who loves truly does it for the sake of love, as the one who is essentially good rejoices in the sake of goodness.

The ones who love are rich for they don't stop giving their best and remain inspired as innate artists. Their compassionate eyes see the beauty of the Beloved all around.

Appreciate, be grateful, love for the sake of that same love, be good for the sake of goodness and you'll grasp the spirit of the Beloved.

RÊVERIE!

I will call you *rêverie*! And you'll feel how the dew drops of my love fall over your hands and taste like honey! I will call you *rêverie* so you know how midsummer's night dreams look like Debussy's *Clair de Lune* tattooed over Tchaikovsky's Swan lake! I will call you *rêverie* and you'll know how the most beautiful melodies conclude in the impromptu of your name!

MANCHESTER IN A VALLEY NOT SO FAR

Everywhere I look I see the memories of the Thames by the Globe Theatre, a Cheshire cat, the cotton tails of deer and strawberry fields of Wonderland.

The Pink Floyd's museum in a window decorated by the country side, a flashback of warming summer promenades, the enchanting green trees like veils for blue skies.

The most beautiful overture for August spectacles of Perseids and Leonids at night. The fields of barley and Manchester in a valley not so far!

HIM: SHOSTAKOVICH'S WALTZ NUMBER 2

There's just one thing equally beautiful to Shostakovich's Waltz number 2! That's a man with an enticing brain. I can feel my curiosity navigating in the infinite waves of his knowledge. A musical sea hiding a plethora of both ancient and apocryphal books, which subversive information would only change humankind. Víctor Hugo taking Kairos by his hair and with it his golden opportunity!

WE'LL GET LOST

We'll get lost as the *tombée du jour* hides the sun in the covers of silky seas! And as we do so, suddenly from God's embrace everything will appear! We'll vanish our thoughts as seraphim's harps do to our fears!

We'll unveil our truth's as Alexandria's books would have done to the history of humankind! For grieving memories, I brought you a poem by Khalil Gibran, I just wanted to remind you how it feels to be one!

Alejandra Rodríguez was born in Bogotá Colombia on August the 11th 1989, she is a Bachelor in Arts of Modern Languages, poet, aerial dancer and holistic therapist. She is the head and founder of *Casa Merkaba*, a place created to promote psychological assistance as well as other alternative therapies and activities that promote self-awareness, empathy and environmental consciousness.

Alejandra writes articles about spiritual awakening and is the co-author of *"Diario del despertar de la Diosa"*, a succinct healing guidebook that fosters fraternity among women worldwide through the mythological experiences of the goddesses, while encouraging them to start an intimate path of healing. This book is also highly recommended to therapists who wish to nurture and vivify their groups or one and one sessions.

Nowadays, Alejandra is working with Adriana Gutiérrez, co-author, holistic therapist, author of 7 books of spiritual literature for children, as well as life coach, in a new guide that helps men to rethink their role in society healing from within.